SONIA'S DIGITAL WORLD

by Shannon McClintock Miller

illustrated by Clara Reschke

PICTURE WINDOW BOOKS

a capstone imprint

Published by Picture Window Books, an imprint of Capstone.
1710 Roe Crest Drive
North Mankato, Minnesota 56003
capstonepub.com

Library of Congress Cataloging-in-Publication Data is available on the Library of Congress website.

ISBN: 9781484687628 (hardcover)
ISBN: 9781484687574 (paperback)
ISBN: 9781484687581 (eBook PDF)

Summary: We are all connected in so many ways! Find out how with a bird's-eye view as Sonia, her friends, and her community chat, create, and play together with digital tools. Follow the virtual trail at home, at school, and all around the world as Sonia, friends, and families make discoveries and connections. Whether face-to-face or far away, find out how Sonia—and you!—are part of the digital world!

Designers: Nathan Gassman and Kayla Rossow

This book is published in partnership with the International Society for Technology in Education (ISTE).

Printed and bound in the USA. 5425

Around your neighborhood and around the world, people are connecting. Learning, playing, talking, working, laughing . . .

There are so many ways to connect!

What devices do you see and use every day?
How do they help you?

Mom, can you record me? I want to show my friends this dance I just learned!

We can stay in touch with family and friends.

We can be part of special events
even if we are far away.

Hey, we've got a
front row seat to Carly's play.
That's really something!

We can solve problems and help others.

Hi!
We're having a bake sale
to raise money for the
local food pantry.

DONATE

DONATE

That's great.
We'd love to help—
and we're hungry!

BALD EAGLE
PRESENTATION
TODAY 1pm

We can all take part.

We can find the answers to millions of questions.

We can share what we know
in all kinds of ways.

We can bring the world home.

There are countless ways we can connect with others!

How will you connect today?

QUESTIONS TO EXPLORE TOGETHER

1. How do you communicate with friends and family who are far away?

2. What digital tools can you use to find answers to your questions, and how do you share knowledge about the fascinating things you learn?

3. How do you work together with others when you're not in the same place?

4. How can you use digital tools to help others in your community and beyond?

5. How do you use technology to learn and create?

I AM A DIGITAL EXPLORER
ISTE STANDARDS

EMPOWERED LEARNER
I use technology to set goals, work toward achieving them, and demonstrate my learning.

GLOBAL COLLABORATOR
I strive to broaden my perspective, understand others, and work effectively in teams using digital tools.

DIGITAL CITIZEN
I understand the rights, responsibilities and opportunities of living, learning, and working in an interconnected digital world.

KNOWLEDGE CONSTRUCTOR
I critically select, evaluate, and synthesize digital resources into a collection that reflects my learning and builds my knowledge.

CREATIVE COMMUNICATOR
I communicate effectively and express myself creatively using different tools, styles, formats, and digital media.

INNOVATIVE DESIGNER
I solve problems by creating new and imaginative solutions using a variety of digital tools.

COMPUTATIONAL THINKER
I identify authentic problems, work with data, and use a step-by-step process to automate solutions.

Tips for Engaging Positively with Technology

- Find a healthy balance between technology use and non-tech activities. Set up guidelines together as a family. Agree on tech-free times, such as family meals, and consider removing devices from bedrooms at the end of the day.

- Make time for family and friends. Take pictures of things you see during a nature hike, create a game or song using an app to share with a friend, or bake with a family member or friend over a video call.

- Together, find a place to help in your community or around the world. Find a Little Free Library (littlefreelibrary.org) on an online map and drop off used books, or use the internet to research ways to help in the community and with global events like Earth Day.

- Find ways to use technology to learn new things and engage with new people. Watch a video to learn how to draw your favorite animal, then share your drawing with a friend or relative. Connect with others in an online art class, coding club, or virtual book club.

- Be thoughtful of when and how you use technology. Use the ISTE Student Standards and Questions to Explore Together to guide your conversations around the use of digital tools. Ensure that everyone—both kids and caregivers—feels empowered and included in the conversation.

About the Author

Shannon McClintock Miller, an international speaker and author, is the PreK-12 district teacher librarian at Van Meter Community School District in Iowa. She also serves as a Future Ready Librarians spokesperson, working with librarians, educators, and students around the world. Shannon is author of the award-winning *The Library Voice* blog, has published two children's book series on libraries and makerspaces with Capstone, and was named a *Library Journal* Mover and Shaker. She earned the Making It Happen Award by ISTE in 2016 and was named the AASL Social Media Superstar Leadership Luminary in 2018. Her most favorite role of all is mom to three amazing kids and lucky wife of Eric.

About the Illustrator

Clara Reschke graduated as a designer at UFSC with a year of study at Cardiff Metropolitan University. Since becoming a professional illustrator, she has illustrated several children's books across Europe, Brazil, and the U.S. She has also worked for the animation industry creating character design and backgrounds. She is currently living by the sea with her partner, her son, and their sweet dog.